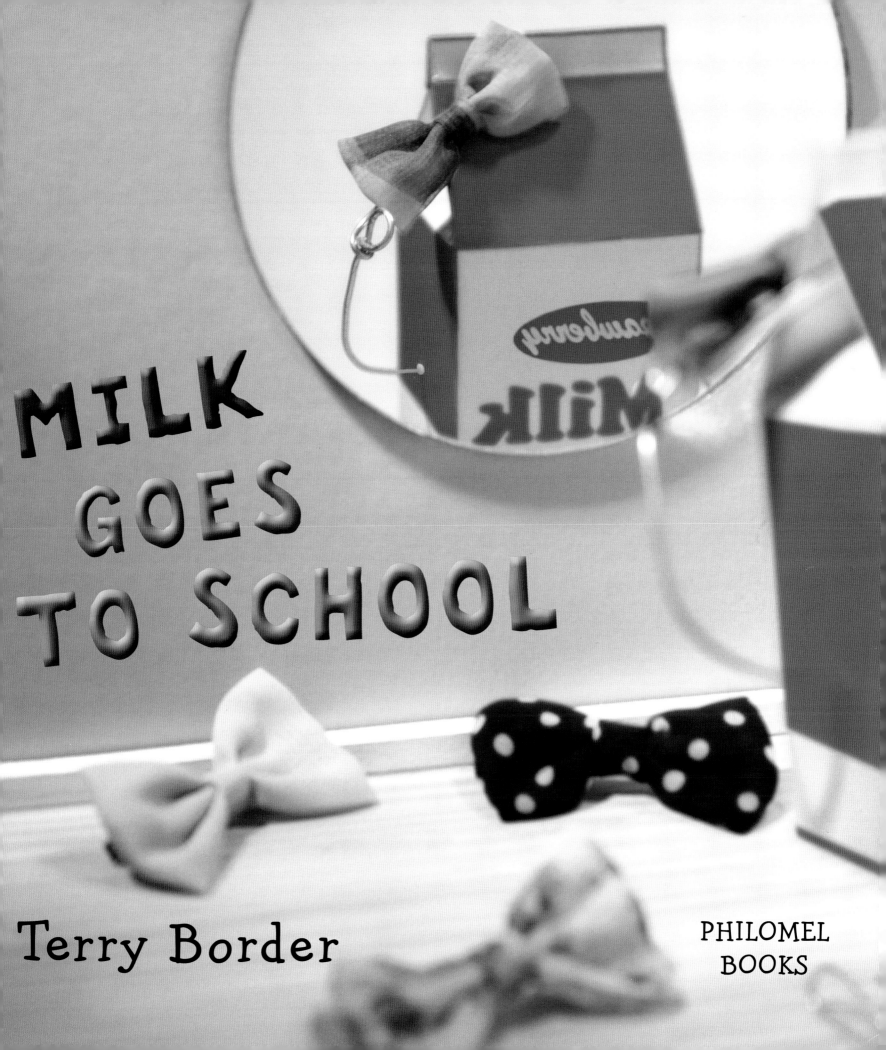

MILK GOES TO SCHOOL

Terry Border

PHILOMEL
BOOKS

PHILOMEL BOOKS

an imprint of Penguin Random House LLC   375 Hudson Street, New York, NY 10014

Philomel Books is a registered trademark of Penguin Random House LLC.

Library of Congress Cataloging-in-Publication Data is available upon request.

Manufactured in China by RR Donnelley Asia Printing Solutions Ltd.   ISBN 978-0-399-17619-7

1 3 5 7 9 10 8 6 4 2

Edited by Jill Santopolo.   Design by Semadar Megged.   Text set in 21.5-point Hank BT.   The art was done by manipulating and photographing three-dimensional objects.

For our daughter, Adeline,
who told us about her day at school every afternoon.
I'm happy she graduated, but I miss those stories!

It was the morning of her first day of school, and Milk was feeling just the tiniest bit scared.

"Don't worry," her dad said. "You're *la crème de la crème*! That means 'the best of the best.'" And he gave her a brand-new backpack for good luck.

At school, Milk walked over to the first kids she saw.
"I really like your backpack," Cupcake said.

"Thank you," Milk answered. "My dad gave it to me. He said I'm 'la crème de la crème'!"

Waffle leaned over to Cupcake and whispered, "I think this Milk is spoiled!"

Milk sniffed herself. She didn't think she was spoiled.

"Please find a seat, everyone," said Miss Pear.
"Sit by me," Milk said to Cupcake. "You're
pretty like I am."
"Yep, she's spoiled!" Waffle said to himself.
But Milk ignored him. She didn't think she
was spoiled at all.

Miss Pear asked everyone to draw a picture of their family.

Milk asked Carrot, "Would you like to share crayons?"

"I don't carrot all," Carrot said. "Like I said to Salad, lettuce be friends!"

Carrot seemed okay.

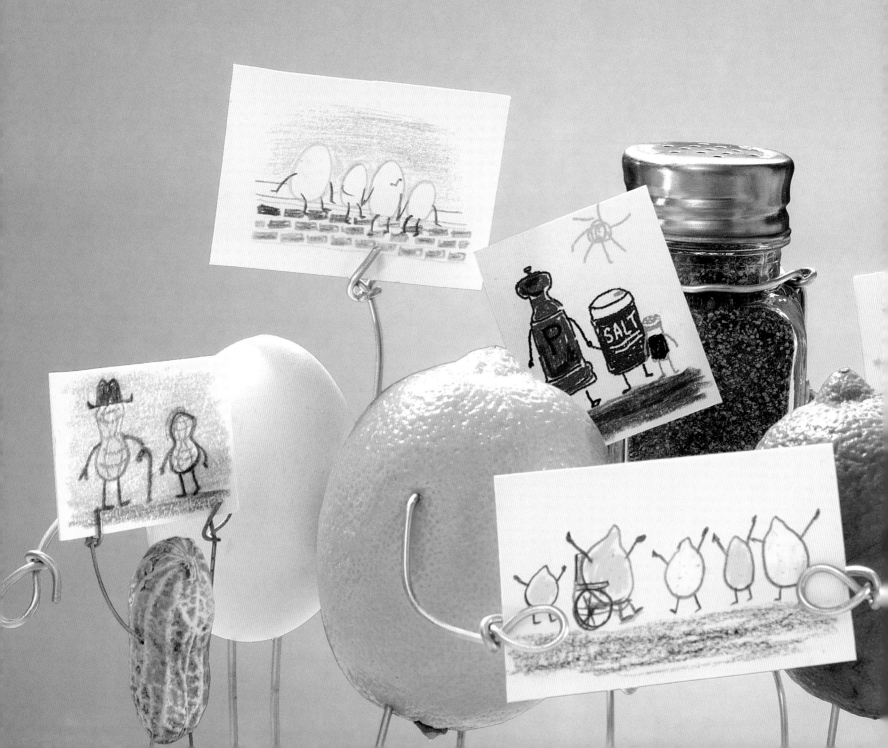

Everyone did a good job, but Milk was really proud
of her drawing.

"Don't you think it looks beautiful?" she
asked Carrot.

Waffle looked at Carrot and said, "Spoiled!"

But Milk shook her head. She didn't think she was
spoiled. She was just trying to be friendly.

Then Miss Pear asked the kids what they wanted to do when they grew up.

Cupcake wanted to be an artist. Peanut wanted to be the first astro-nut on Mars.

Potato wanted to be a
sailor on a gravy boat.

Milk said that maybe she
could be a queen, because
she liked being the boss.

Waffle said, "She's so spoiled!"
"You don't seem too sweet yourself!" said Milk.

Next, the class worked on their spelling.
Milk couldn't wait to show the other kids
what a good speller she was.

So when Milk's paper got splattered, she yelled and stomped her feet. "You messed it up, Soup!" she said.

Waffle turned to Soup and said—

"She's spoiled!"

But Milk didn't think she was spoiled. She just liked having her paper look pretty, is all.

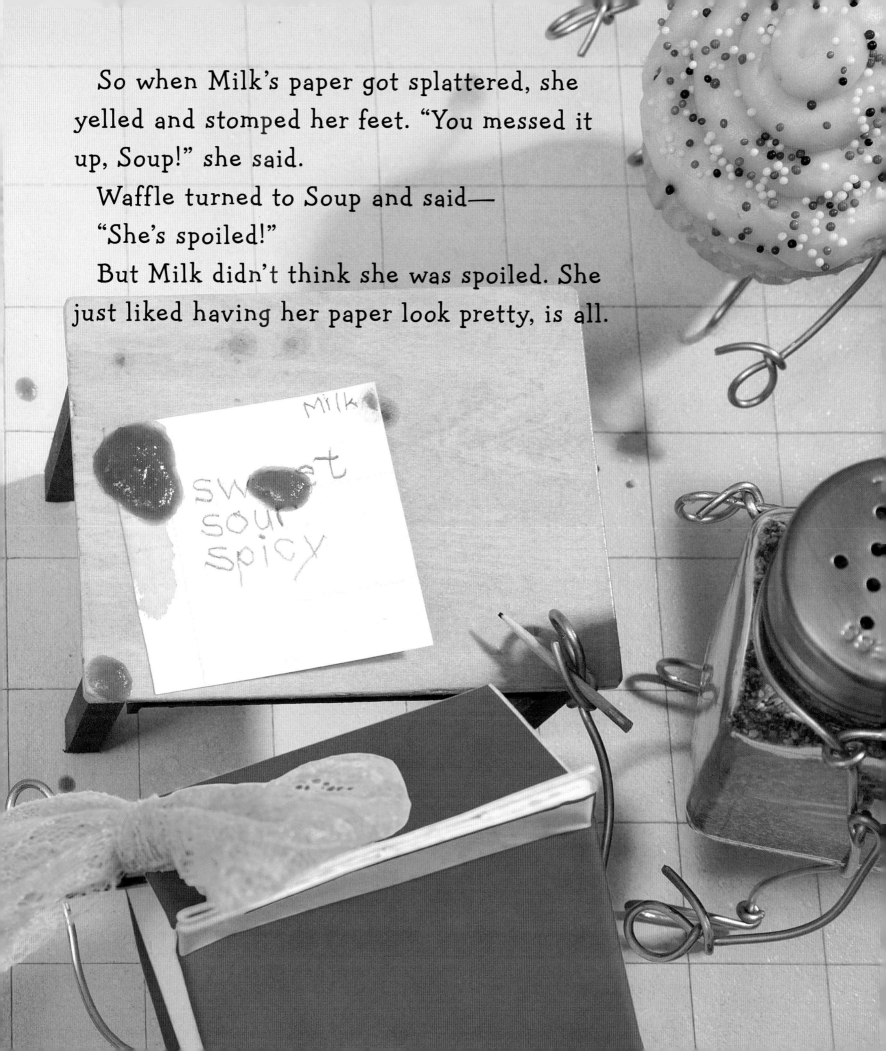

Later, in the library, Milk asked if someone cut the cheese.

"I don't like that saying," said Cheese, "but I think someone tooted."

"Oops. Sorry," said Beans.
Milk started to leave. "I'll curdle if I stay."
"Spoiled!" Waffle mouthed to Beans.
"You don't seem too sweet yourself!" said Milk.
"You're an awful waffle!"

On the way back to class, Milk followed Waffle and
Cupcake in line.

"Waffle, you are slower than syrup," said Milk.

"That's not true," said Waffle. "Syrup is way back
there behind us."

Cupcake turned and waved at him.

Milk was not happy. She was just trying to be friendly.

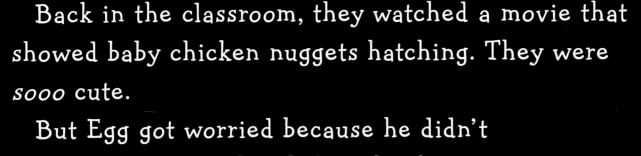

Back in the classroom, they watched a movie that showed baby chicken nuggets hatching. They were *sooo* cute.

But Egg got worried because he didn't want something to hatch from him!

Milk said, "Don't worry, I think you might be a rotten egg!"

"Look who's talking!" answered Egg, and then both of them got in trouble for arguing.

"They're both spoiled," Waffle said to Cupcake.

Milk decided she did not like Waffle.

At recess, Milk watched as Apple asked Waffle how they could get some more kids to play tag.

"I SCREAM!" yelled Waffle.
"Really?" Apple said. "Why would you do that?"
"I SCREAM!" yelled Waffle.
"I know! I heard you," said Apple, "and it's scaring me!"

Waffle said, "I'm just trying to get Ice Cream's attention over there. Ice Cream! Hey, Ice Cream! Would you like to play?"

Milk wished someone would invite her to play. But she knew what Waffle would say if she asked. And Milk didn't think she was spoiled at all!

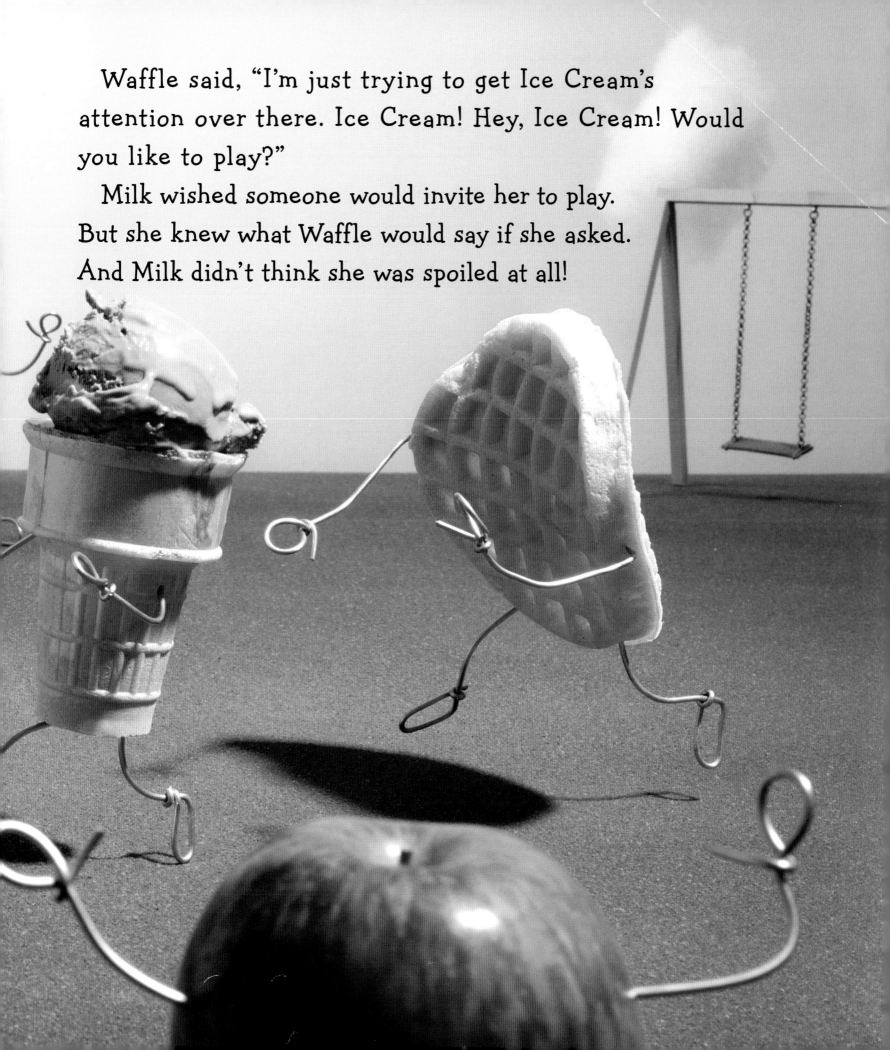

At the end of recess, Celery lost a raisin, and everyone helped look for it. After a while, Milk admitted she had already thrown it away when she

found it sticking to her shoe. She did offer to get him a
new one. But Waffle rolled his eyes.

Milk wasn't sure if she liked school at all. Or if any of
the kids liked her.

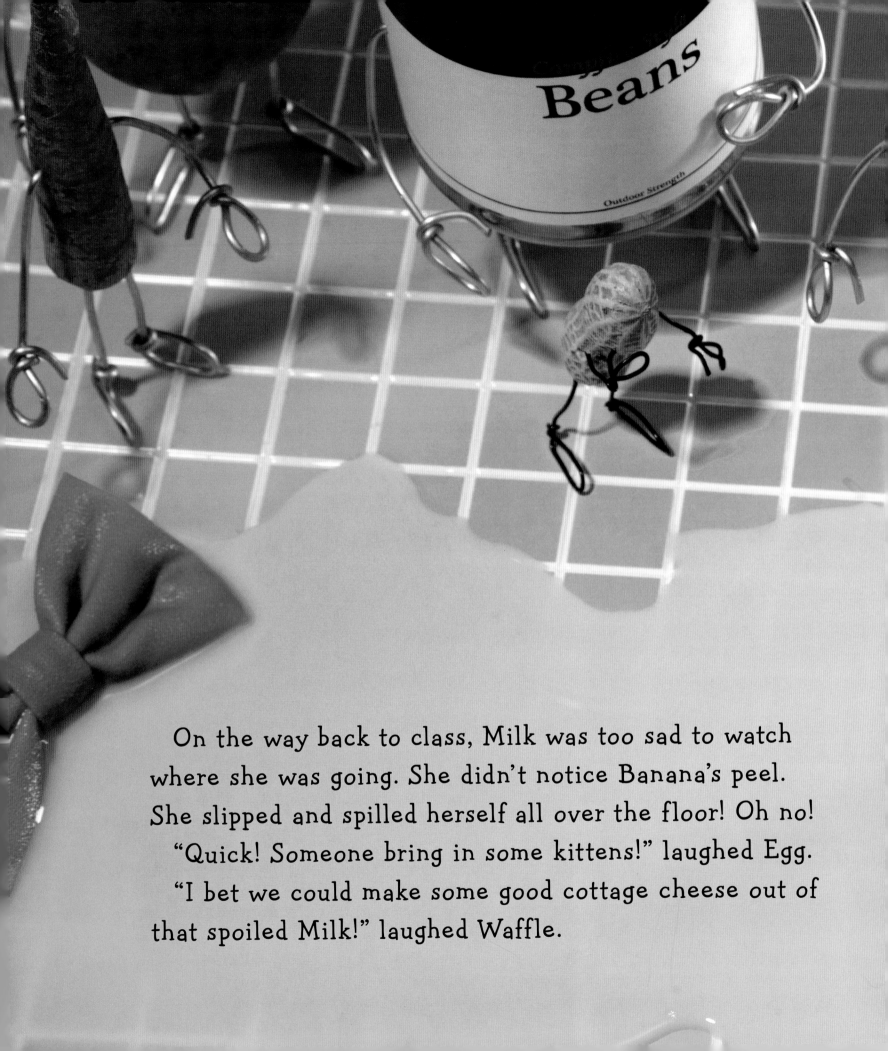

On the way back to class, Milk was too sad to watch where she was going. She didn't notice Banana's peel. She slipped and spilled herself all over the floor! Oh no! "Quick! Someone bring in some kittens!" laughed Egg. "I bet we could make some good cottage cheese out of that spoiled Milk!" laughed Waffle.

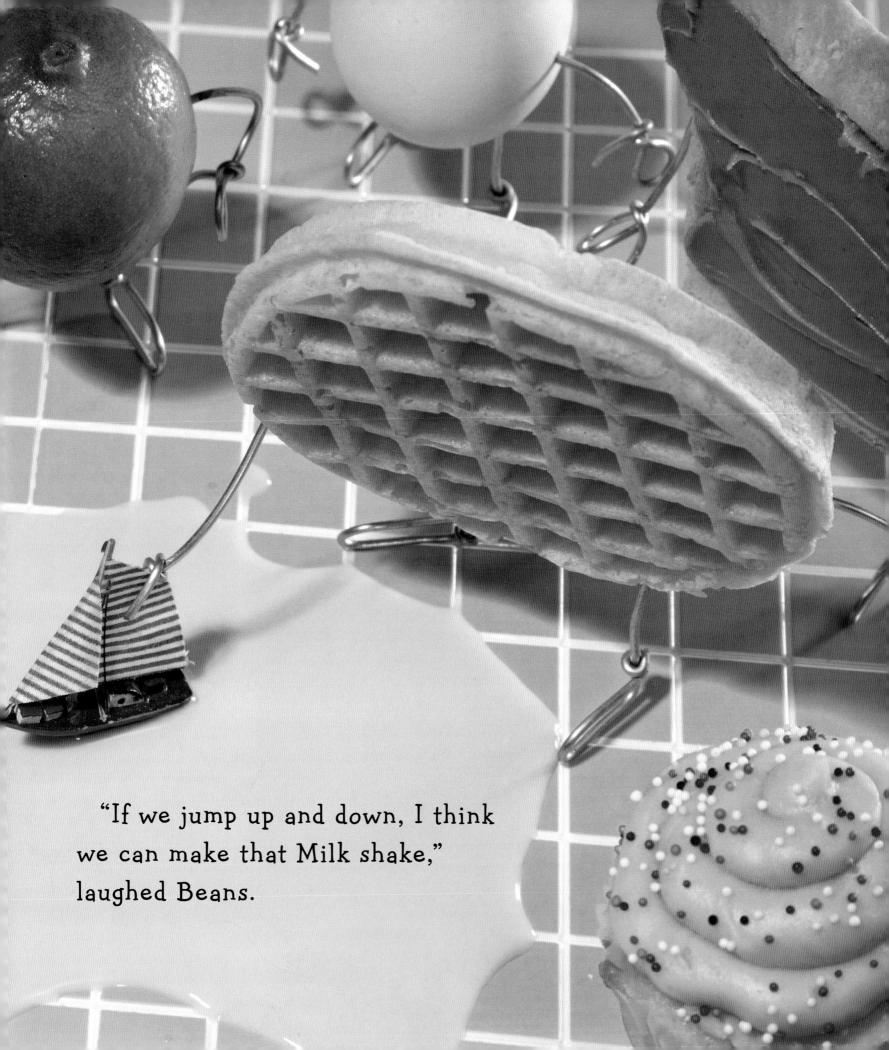

"If we jump up and down, I think we can make that Milk shake," laughed Beans.

Cupcake was worried and began to cry. "Milk might be a little spoiled, but she *did* ask me to sit by her this morning."

"And when we drew pictures, she did share her best crayons," said Carrot.

"Plus, she said she would go to the lunchroom to get me a new raisin," said Celery.

"And Milk does help grow strong teeth and bones!" said Barbecue Chicken.

"Let's not cry over spilled Milk!" said Miss Pear. "We'll mop her up and get her back in her carton in no time."

During all of this, while she was just a big puddle, Milk heard her classmates. She was surprised any of them cared about her, especially because maybe she *had* been acting a little bit—just the tiniest bit—spoiled.

But the excitement wasn't over for the day. As soon as
Milk was back in her carton and all the kids were back
in the classroom, Cupcake got a whiff of Pepper, who
was standing nearby, and—"Aaaaah-aaaah-aaaah-CHOO!"
Cupcake sneezed off her frosting and sprinkles . . . all
over Milk and everyone else in the class!

"Oops!" said Cupcake.

Everyone waited for Milk to get steamed, but she
didn't yell or stamp her feet.

"It's okay, Cupcake, it was an accident," said Milk.
"Now we all look like la crème de la crème."

The whole class laughed. Even Waffle.

"I was wrong about you," Waffle said to Milk.
"You're not *too* spoiled."

"That's nice of you to say," said Milk. "You
actually seem pretty sweet yourself."